This Little Princess

story belongs to

. . . .

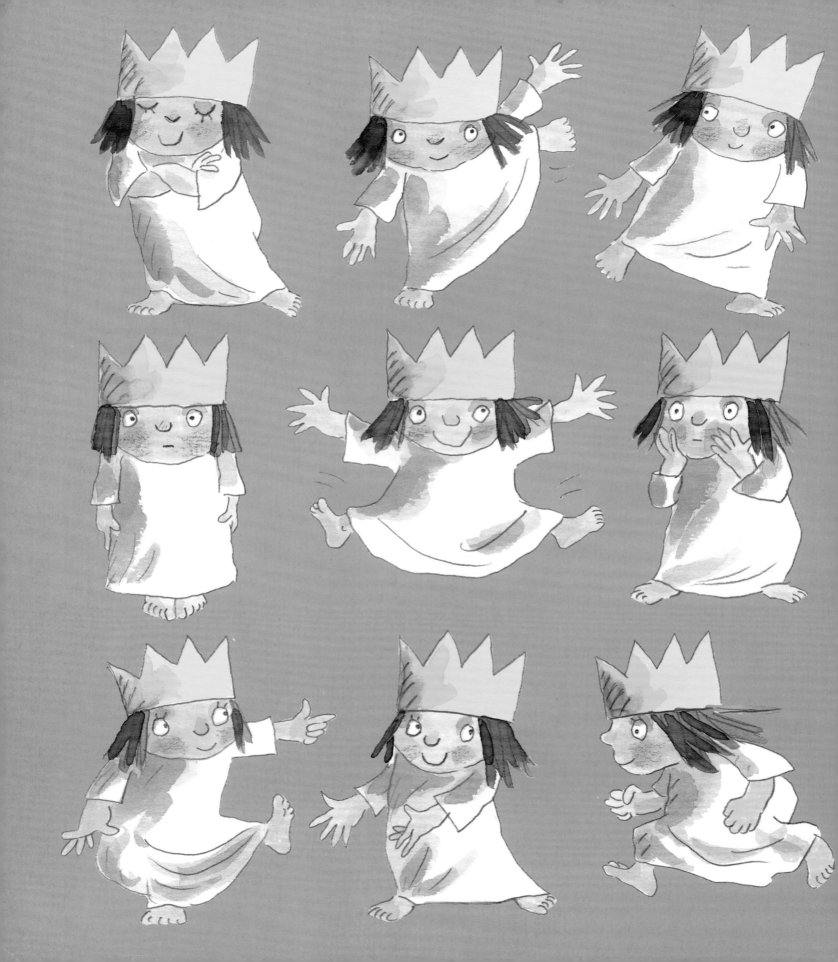

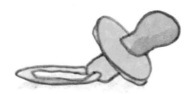

This paperback edition published in 2012 by Andersen Press Ltd.

Published in Australia by Random House Australia Pty., Level 3, 100 Pacific Highway, North Sydney, NSW 2060.

First published in Great Britain in 2001 by Andersen Press Ltd.

Text and Illustration copyright © Tony Ross, 2001

Colour separated in Switzerland by Photolitho AG, Zürich.

Printed and bound in China by Foshan Zhao Rong Printing Co., Ltd.

Tony Ross has used pen, ink and watercolour in this book.

10   9   8   7   6   5   4   3   2

British Library Cataloguing in Publication Data available.

ISBN 978 1 84939 380 5 (Trade paperback edition)
ISBN 978 1 78344 015 3 (Riverside edition)

A Little Princess Story

I Want My Dummy!

Tony Ross

Andersen Press

"I want my dummy!"

"You're not still using a dummy?" said the Admiral.
"It's nice!" said the Little Princess.

"This tastes much better than a dummy," said the Cook.
"No, it doesn't!" said the Little Princess.

"Where's my dummy gone?"

". . . I want my dummy!"

"How did it get up the chimney?"

"I'll never lose it again!"

"Where's my dummy? I want my dummy!"

"What's it doing under the dog?" said the Little Princess.

"I'll NEVER lose my dummy again!" she said.

"NEVER, never, never, never . . ."

"Burglars have taken my dummy! I want my dummy!"

"How did it get into the dustbin?"

"It tastes better after a wash!" said the Little Princess.

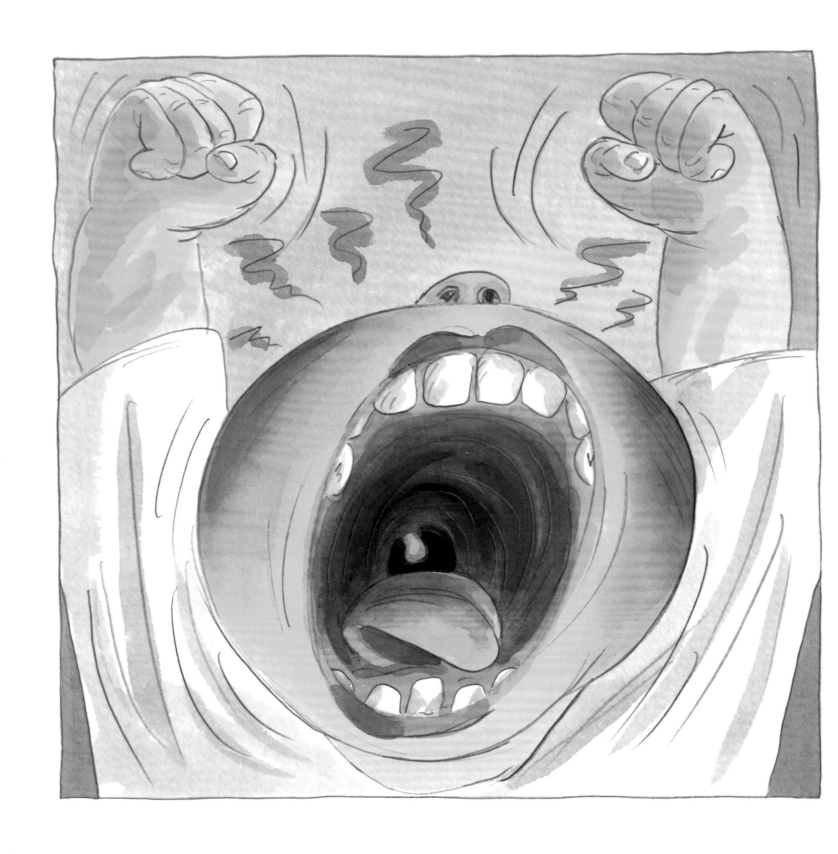

"It's gone again! I WANT MY DUMMY!"

"How did it get into the pond?"

"I'll never let it go again!" said the Little Princess.
"It's safe on this ribbon."

"Aren't you too grown-up for a dummy?" said the Prime Minister.
"No!" said the Little Princess.

"Soldiers don't have dummies!" said the General.
"Ladies don't have dummies, either," said the Maid.

"Well I do, SO THERE!" said the Little Princess.

"That dummy looks stupid!" said her cousin.

"It does!" said the Little Princess.
"But it's not mine . . ."

"...it's Ted's!"

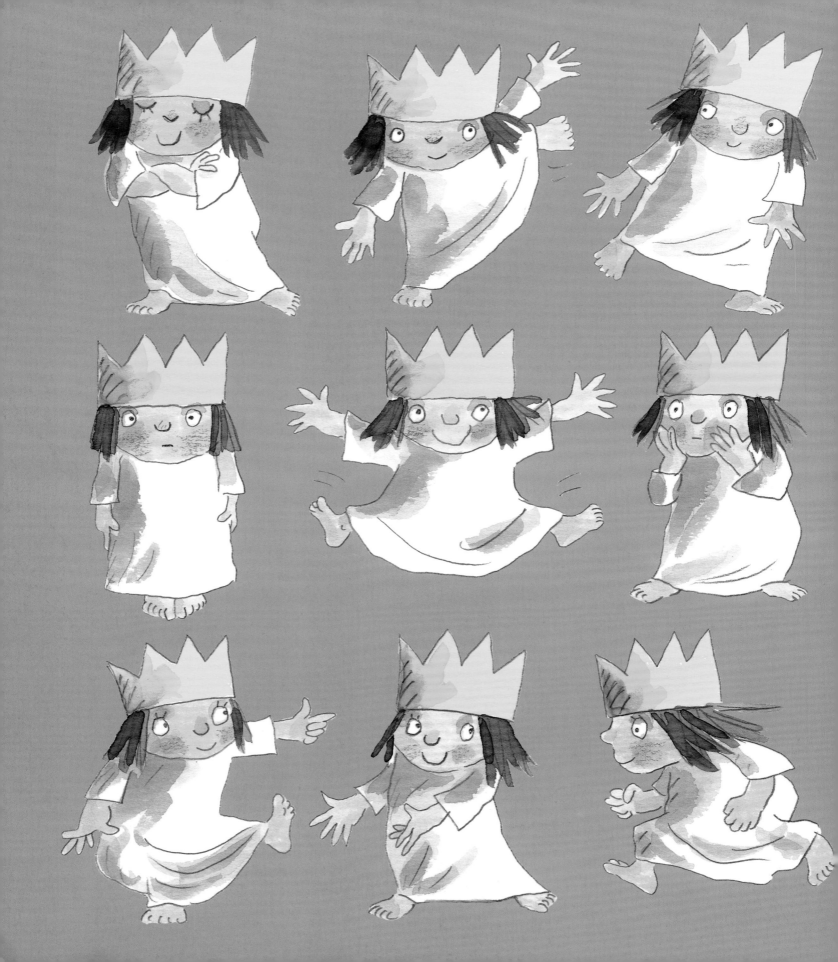

Other Little Princess Books

I Didn't Do it!

I Don't Want to Go to Hospital!

I Don't Want to Wash My Hands!

I Want a Boyfriend!

I Want a Party!

I Want a Sister!

I Want My Dummy!

I Want My Light On!

I Want My Potty!

I Want to Be!

I Want to Do it By Myself!

I Want to Go Home!

I Want to Win!

I Want Two Birthdays!

Little Princess titles are also available as eBooks.

LITTLE PRINCESS TV TIE-INS

Fun in the Sun!

I Want to Do Magic!

I Want My Sledge!

I Don't Like Salad!

I Don't Want to Comb My Hair!

I Want to Go to the Fair!

I Want to Be a Cavegirl!

I Want to Be Tall!

I Want My Sledge! Book and DVD